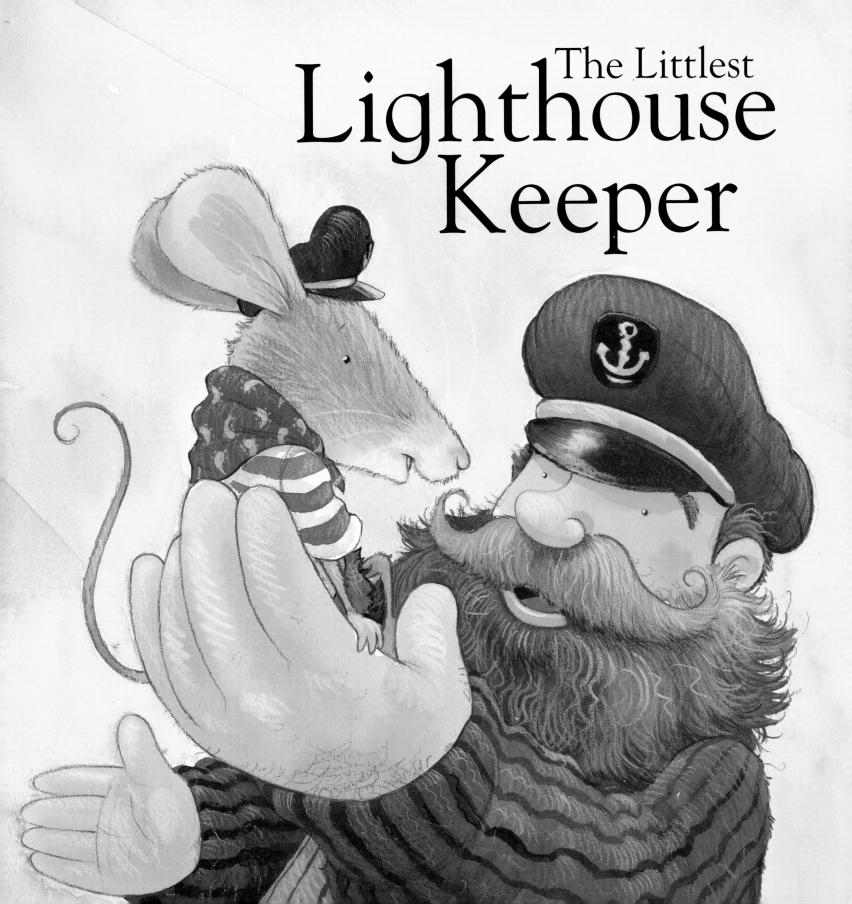

The Littlest
Lighthouse
Keeper

Author Heidi Howarth
Illustrator Daniel Howarth
Editor Clare Weaver
Designer Alix Wood
Consultant Anne Faundez

Publisher Steve Evans
Creative Director Zeta Davies

Sandy Creek
122 Fifth Avenue
New York, NY 10011

ISBN 978 1 4351 1658 0

Library of Congress Control Number: 2008011790

Printed and bound in China

10 9 8 7 6 5 4 3 2 1

The Littlest
Lighthouse
Keeper

Heidi and
Daniel Howarth

SANDY CREEK

Henry loved to be by the sea.
He loved the smell and the
sound of the ocean.

He lived in a lighthouse by
the bay and helped the old
lighthouse keeper.

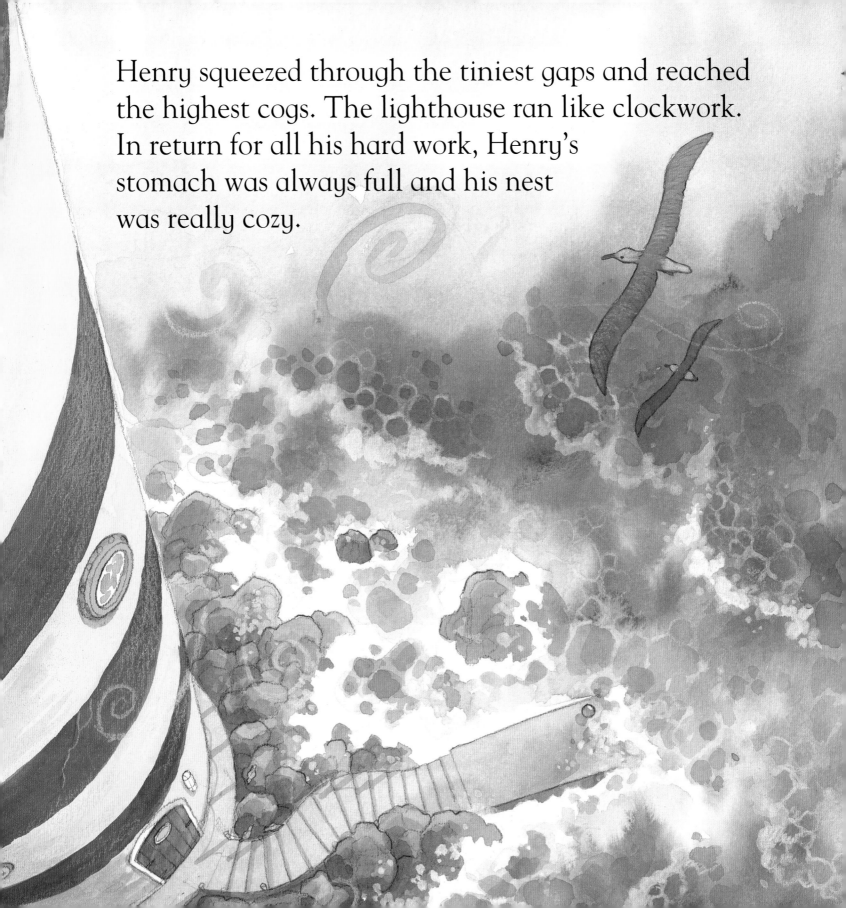

Henry squeezed through the tiniest gaps and reached the highest cogs. The lighthouse ran like clockwork. In return for all his hard work, Henry's stomach was always full and his nest was really cozy.

Today, Henry had been busy at work all morning when he noticed something. The lighthouse was quiet. The only sound was the tick tock of the old keeper's clock.

Henry scampered downstairs.

The lighthouse keeper had gone.
All he had left was a note saying
"Gone to the dentist!"

But he had
forgotten one very
important thing.
Henry could
not read.

Henry climbed sadly back to his nest.
Tap… Tap… Tap!
A puffin was tapping on the glass.

"Are you hungry?" she asked.
"I wasn't sure if you ate fish like
me, so I brought you this."

Henry pushed open the window.
What a feast—berries, nuts, and seeds.

"Oh, thank you," said Henry.
"This is perfect. I was so hungry."

With a full stomach
and a new friend,
Henry returned
to his chores.

There was one job Henry had never tried on his own. He had always sat safe in the keeper's pocket as the old man climbed the steep ladder to the top of the lighthouse.

"I can do this," Henry said to himself.

Looking up, it all
seemed so scary.
Henry's paws were
trembling… they
slipped and Arrrrrrh!
Henry fell.

Henry's eyes were tightly shut… he was scared
to open them. He felt he was floating.
 "Hello," said a gentle voice.
Henry slowly opened one eye. There was
a spider, with big beadlike eyes.

"My web caught you," she said.
"Where were you going?"

"To the lamp at the top of the lighthouse,"
Henry replied. "I need to check it is working."
"I will climb with you," said Spider.

Henry was still chatting to his new friend as he reached the top. The sky had grown dark and a ship was sounding its horn.

"I need to switch it on," cried Henry.

"What?" asked Spider.

"The light!" Henry called. "It will guide the ship!"

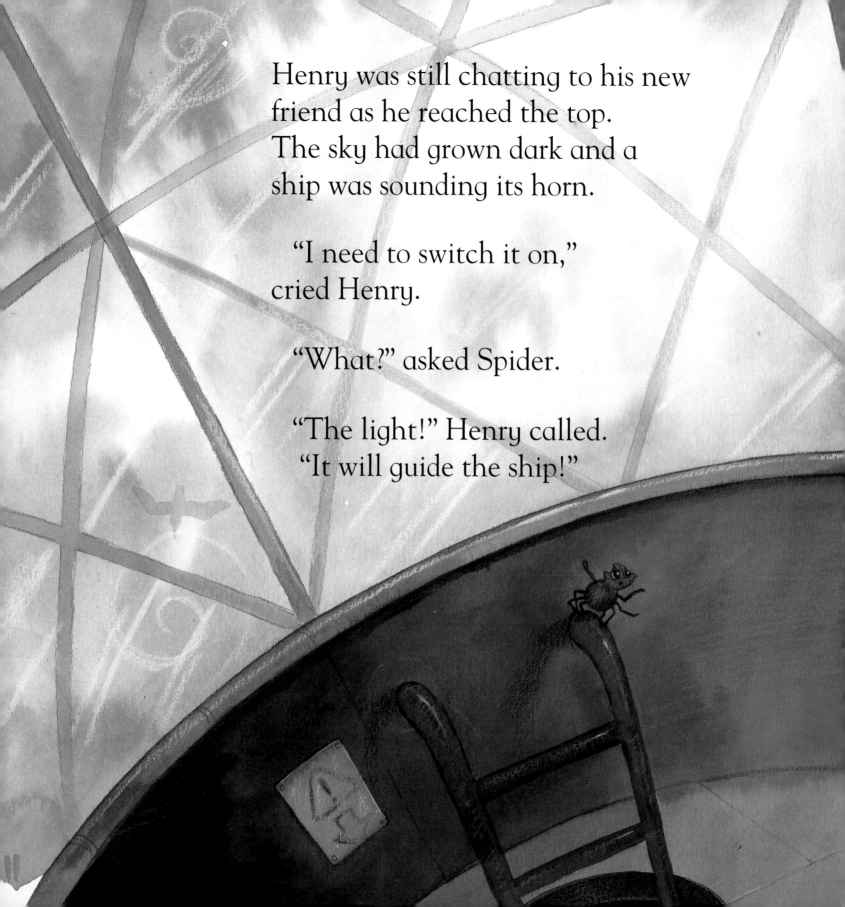

Henry pulled and pulled as
hard as he could… CLICK!

Nothing happened.
The lighthouse was still dark.
Henry turned off the switch.

Henry knew there was a spare bulb, but it was right at the bottom of the lighthouse and he was at the top. There was no time to fetch it.

Spider seemed to have gone and with no lighthouse keeper to help, what could Henry do?

Suddenly, Henry heard a sound.
Puffin fluttered above him, with Spider
dangling from a silvery strand.

"Come on," said Spider, "I have
a plan that might just work and
I have brought some help."

The plan was simple. Henry and Spider climbed onto Puffin's back and down she flew. Spider spun a web and they put the spare bulb safely in it.

Quickly, they hopped back onto Puffin and off she flew to the top of the lighthouse.

Spider and Henry hopped to the floor. Henry took out the old bulb and screwed the new bulb into place.

What had seemed impossible for Henry on his own had been easy for the three friends working together. They smiled.

Henry pulled the switch.
A bright beam of light
shone out across the bay.

"We did it!" cried Henry.

The friends cheered as they watched the ship sail safely away from the sharp rocks below.

Henry was so tired he did not know he had fallen asleep until his nose twitched with a delicious smell… Sizzling bacon!

"Hello Henry," said a familiar voice.
"I am so sorry to have left you."
"What a wonderful job you have done," he said.
"You may be the littlest lighthouse keeper but you make a really big difference."

He gave Henry a special little lighthouse keeper's cap, and he didn't forget Henry's new friends either.

Spider could spin her webs wherever she wanted and Puffin had fresh fish to eat every day.

But best of all they all had each other.